AT SEASIDE COTTAGE

A collection of thirteen everyday stories
by one of the most famous writers for
children.

These stories are just the right length for
bedtime reading, and include many of
the experiences of day-to-day life which
are comfortingly familiar to the young
child.

Cover by Roger Payne

Enid Blyton

At Seaside Cottage

Illustrated by Caroline Sharpe

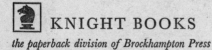

KNIGHT BOOKS
the paperback division of Brockhampton Press

SBN 340 04218 4

*This collection first published 1969 by Knight Books,
the paperback division of Brockhampton Press Ltd, Leicester*

*Printed and bound in Great Britain by
Cox & Wyman Ltd, London, Reading and Fakenham*

*Text copyright © 1969 Enid Blyton
Illustrations copyright © 1969 Brockhampton Press Ltd*

Contents

The three sailors

PETER, Rosemary and Richard were staying by the sea. Their house was almost on the beach. It was lovely. Every day they had tea on the beach, and Granny, Mummy and Daddy came too.

Granny didn't like sitting on the sand, so Daddy had brought down a chair and a wooden table from the house for her. Mummy had a tablecloth, and Granny sat up to the table and poured out tea and milk for everyone.

After tea the children wanted to go out in a boat.

'No,' said Daddy. 'Not today. I want to finish my book. Besides, the sea is too rough today. You wouldn't like going in a boat.'

'Oh, Daddy, we should, we should!' said Peter. 'We are such good sailors. Can't we go in a boat by ourselves? We could manage it quite all right.'

'Certainly not!' said Daddy.

So the three children had to be good and dig castles in the sand. Granny helped them. She gave them bits of coloured wool too, to put among the seaweed for flowers when they made a garden for the castle.

'Perhaps Daddy will take you in a boat to-morrow,' she said.

The next day the sea was just as rough, but the children ran to ask their father to get a boat.

'No, the sea is still too rough,' Daddy said. 'You might be sea-sick.'

'Oh, Daddy, we wouldn't be, really and truly!' said Richard. 'We are such good sailors. Do take us! Oh, do get a boat and let us go out in it!'

But Daddy wouldn't. He said they could none of them swim well enough to go out in a boat on a rough sea.

'I'm sure I could swim all right if I fell out of a boat,' said Rosemary, sulking.

Then Daddy got cross and said nobody was to mention boats again till he did. So the three children set to work to dig, though they all looked rather sulky.

It was Granny who thought of a good idea

for them. 'Why don't you turn the wooden table upside down and pretend it's a boat?' she said. 'That would be fun. You could tie the tablecloth to Daddy's stick and tie that to one of the table legs, and you would have a mast and sail. Your spades can be oars.'

'Oooh, yes! We'll play pirates!' cried Richard in excitement. 'Come and help, you others.'

The table was quickly turned upside down, and Richard began to tie Daddy's stick to a leg for a mast. Then Rosemary tied the tablecloth to the stick, and the wind flapped it out for a fine sail. It was most exciting!

'Daddy and Granny and I are going for a walk this afternoon till tea-time,' said Mummy. 'We will bring tea down with us when we come back. Amuse yourselves well and have a nice afternoon, all of you.'

The three children were left on the beach alone. They were pleased. Now they could play pirates and shout all they wanted to. What a fine boat the big wooden table made!

They got the cushions out of the chairs in the house and put them in the upside-down table.

They got their spades for oars. The sail flapped merrily in the breeze.

'Yo-ho for a life on the ocean wave!' shouted Peter. 'We'll have some fine adventures!'

They did! They sailed after ships and caught them. They took prisoners. They had a wreck. They did enjoy their game, and at last they were so hot and tired that they didn't want to play any more.

'I'm going to have a rest,' said Peter, flopping down on a cushion in the upside-down table.

'So am I,' said Rosemary, fanning herself.

'Let's pretend that we are drifting off to a wonderful treasure island!' said Richard. 'Ship your oars, everyone! While we rest, our ship will take us to a wonderful land where we can find hidden treasure.'

They all lay down on the cushions and shut their eyes. The sun shone down. It was lovely and hot. The little breeze cooled them nicely. In two minutes all three children were fast asleep.

Now the tide was coming in very fast, with the wind behind it. A big wave ran right up the beach and lapped against the table. The

children didn't see it. They were fast asleep, of course. Another wave came, and another. Each one ran up to the table. A bigger wave still ran all round it.

Then such a big wave came that it lifted the table up! Then two more waves ran underneath and took that upside-down table and floated it gently out to sea.

Richard's feet were in the water but he didn't notice it. Rosemary's hair hung over the side of the table and got wet, but she was fast asleep. Peter's spade floated off by itself.

The sea was pleased with its boat. It bobbed it up and down, up and down – and suddenly a wave splashed right over the table and woke all three children up with a jump!

They sat up in a hurry. How astonished they were to find themselves out at sea on their table! The beach looked a long, long way away.

'Oooh! Our table's a real boat!' said Peter, looking scared.

'The sea has taken it away!' said Rosemary.

'We wanted to go out in a boat by ourselves and now we have,' said Richard, not liking it at all.

'I feel sick,' said Peter, holding on to the table, for it was bobbing up and down tremendously on the waves.

'So do I,' said Rosemary.

'I feel frightened,' said Richard, beginning to cry. 'We can't swim enough to save ourselves.'

'I told Daddy I could, but I daren't,' said Rosemary.

'Oh, what shall we do?' cried Richard. 'I'm scared!'

The three poor sailors clung to the bobbing table for all they were worth. The tablecloth sail flapped merrily. The cushions were soaked every time a big wave broke on the table.

'We shall be drowned!' said Peter, looking very white.

'If only someone would rescue us!' cried Richard, his tears tasting as salt as the sea-spray.

'Look! There's Daddy coming down to the beach with the tea things!' said Rosemary.

'Yell as loud as you can,' said Peter.

So they yelled, 'Dad-dee, Dad-dee, Dad-dee!'

Their father was looking round the beach in

surprise, seeing no children. Then he suddenly heard their voices and looked out to sea. How astonished he was to see the three sailors on the table!

'Save us, Daddy, save us!' shouted Peter.

Do you know what Daddy did? He began to laugh and laugh and laugh.

'So you are three sailors after all!' he shouted. 'How do you like it?'

'Oh, Daddy, save us!' shouted Rosemary.

'You silly children, jump into the water and wade to shore with the table!' yelled Daddy.

'Daddy, we shall be drowned!' wept Richard. 'The sea is so deep!'

'Peter! Jump out and wade to shore!' shouted Daddy again. 'Go on, do as I tell you. I'm not going to wet my nice white trousers to come and fetch you in.'

Peter put one leg over the table into the sea. He clung hard to the table-leg and let himself go into the water. Splash!

What a surprise for him! Although he was so far out from shore the sea was only up to his knees. It took a long time for the sea to get really deep there, for the tide flowed in over level sand.

'Oh! We can paddle back,' said Peter in surprise. 'I'm only up to my knees. Get out, Rosemary, and help.'

Rosemary jumped out. Then Richard jumped too, and together the three sailors paddled back to the beach, dragging their table behind them.

'Well, well, well!' said Daddy, still laughing. 'Who's going to worry me to take them out in a boat on a rough sea again?'

Nobody said a word. Nobody wanted to go out in a boat on the rough sea now. The three sailors were rather ashamed of themselves. But Granny and Mummy were quite excited to hear about the adventure, so they all cheered up, put the table the right way up for Granny, and had a lovely tea.

Julia's nest

'THE birds are all making their nests,' said Julia. 'Look, Mummy, there's a sparrow with a feather in his beak. He's taking it to tuck into his nest somewhere, isn't he?'

'I expect so,' said Mummy. 'And there's another bird with a piece of straw, Julia. They are all very busy with their nests just now.'

'How can they make them if they haven't any hands?' said Julia. 'They only have their beaks. They don't use their legs to build nests with, do they?'

'Oh, no,' said Mummy. 'Only their beaks. They are very clever with them. They tuck the bits and pieces in here and there, and make the lovely nests you see in every hedgerow. It's a great shame when somebody pulls them to pieces, because it takes a bird quite a long time to build its nest.'

'I shall make one myself,' said Julia. 'I ought

to be able to make a very, very good one because I have two hands, with fingers and thumbs. Now let me see, what do I want for a nest?'

'Little twigs, bits of hay, root fibres, moss, dead leaves, hair, feathers – things like that,' said her mother.

'I'll make a lovely nest,' said Julia. 'And I'll put it in the middle of the hawthorn hedge, and then if any bird has its own nest spoilt it can have mine. I'm sure all the birds will see me making it and will know it is for any of them that needs a new nest.'

She went out into the garden. She found plenty of tiny twigs, and she took some heather stems, because they were nice and thin and wiry – easy to weave together for a nest.

She found it much more difficult than she had thought it would be. 'The little bits won't stay together,' she said. 'They won't make a nice round nest. It looks untidy. I believe that one beak is better than two hands after all!'

Still, it did begin to look like a nest after a bit. Julia stuffed some dead leaves into the cracks and trimmed it up with moss. It began to look very nice.

'How do I make it nice and round and cup-shaped inside?' she asked her mother. 'What does the bird do to make it like a cup inside?'

'Oh, it just gets in and turns itself round and round a little,' said Mummy. 'It soon becomes cup-shaped then.'

Julia put her little fist gently into the nest and turned it round a little. 'It's making a nice round place inside!' she cried. 'Look – just like a real nest, Mummy!'

'It looks lovely,' said Mummy. 'I think you have made it very well, Julia.'

'Oh, I do wish some bird would come and lay its eggs in my nest,' said Julia. 'Do you think one will?'

'I shouldn't think so,' said Mummy. 'Birds like to make their own nests, you know.'

No birds came to live in Julia's nest, though two or three sparrows, a robin and a thrush came and had a good look at it. Julia was disappointed. Her nest stayed in the hawthorn bush, quite empty.

Then one day she came rushing to her mother. 'Mummy! A dreadful thing's happened! You know the nest the robin made on the bank at the bottom of the garden – the one quite near the hedge where I put my nest? Well, somebody or something has pulled the robin's nest all to pieces – and oh, Mummy, the eggs are gone too. The little robins are dreadfully unhappy.'

'Oh, dear,' said Mummy. 'Surely no child has been cruel enough to pull a robin's nest to pieces. It must have been done by a rat.'

She went down the garden with Julia. Sure enough, there was the poor little nest, all pulled to pieces and scattered everywhere. There was no sign of the four red-brown eggs that the little robins had been so proud of.

'Look at the poor robins,' said Julia, crying. 'They simply don't know what to do. They keep flying round and calling out. They don't know where to look for their eggs.'

'The rat has eaten them,' said Mummy sadly. 'I'm afraid it was a rat.'

'Will the robins use my nest now?' said Julia, wiping her eyes.

'I shouldn't think so,' said Mummy. 'You see, robins like to build somewhere low down, not high up on a hedge.'

'I shall watch and see,' said Julia. So she

stayed to watch, and that afternoon she suddenly began to feel excited. The robins flew up into the hedge and looked at the nest she had made.

I believe they're going to have it for their new one, she thought. I do believe they are. Then they will lay eggs in it and I shall have baby birds in my very own nest.

But to her great disappointment they didn't use her nest. Instead they began to pull it to pieces. Julia was surprised and sad.

Oh! They knew how sad they were when they had their own nest pulled to bits, and now they're pulling mine to bits, thought Julia. They're horrid!

She ran to tell her mother. Mummy came down the garden to see. Then she turned to Julia with a smile.

'Julia,' she said, 'they are certainly pulling your nest to pieces, but they are going to use all the bits to make another nest for themselves! What do you think of that? See, they are flying down to the ditch below the hawthorn hedge, with twigs and leaves in their beaks. They are saving themselves the trouble

of hunting for nesting material. They are going to use all the stuff you collected!'

And that is exactly what the little red-breasted couple did. They used Julia's twigs and heather stems and leaves and moss and hair and feathers for a perfectly new nest just below the hedge. Julia was so pleased. She stayed and watched them all the time and they didn't mind a bit.

Now they have laid four more eggs in their new nest, and they always seem very pleased indeed when Julia comes to have a look.

'She won't hurt us,' they sing to one another. 'She found all the stuff for this nest. She's a friend, a friend, a friend!'

Grandad's armchair

ONE day the twins, Simon and Sally, went to ask Mrs Straws, the farmer's wife, for twelve new-laid eggs.

'You can each take a basket,' said Mummy, 'and bring back six, and that will be twelve altogether. Don't run when you bring the eggs back, in case you fall over and break them.'

Off went the twins, swinging a little basket each. They liked going to the farm. They liked all the clucking hens, the quacking ducks, and the little skippetty lambs with their mothers.

They came to the farm and knocked at the door. Mrs Straws opened it. 'Good morning, my dears,' she said. 'I suppose you've come for the eggs. Well, now, step inside a minute and I'll go and get them for you.'

They went into the big kitchen. It always smelt so nice. Sally sniffed. 'It smells of all the nice cakes you've ever baked, and of apple pudding and sausage rolls!' she said. 'I do like your kitchen.'

Mrs Straws laughed. 'I'm going to the hen-house for the eggs,' she said. 'Old Grandad is in the next room. If he calls for anything, go and see what he wants, will you?'

'Yes, Mrs Straws,' said Simon, hoping that Old Grandad *wouldn't* call.

Mrs Straws went out, and no sooner had she shut the door behind her than there came a shout from the next room.

'Annie! Annie! I want you!'

'He's calling Mrs Straws,' said Sally. 'Oh dear, he sounds a bit cross.'

'We'll have to go and see what he wants,' said Simon, and the two of them went into the next room. A big, red-faced man sat in an enormous armchair. He had whiskers all round his chin, and very bright blue eyes.

'Hallo, who are you?' he said. 'Where's my granddaughter, Annie?'

'Gone to get some new-laid eggs, sir,' said Simon politely. 'Can we get you something? Mrs Straws said we were to see what you wanted, if you shouted.'

'Well, I want you to get my spectacles for me,' said Old Grandad. 'I had them on my knee a minute ago, and now I can't find them any-where! Bless my soul, I don't know where things go to! I lost my pencil yesterday, and my knife last week, and . . .'

'Goodness! Wherever do you put them?' said Sally.

'Nowhere! I've got a bad leg and I can't get out of this chair,' said Old Grandad. 'But Annie, she hunts all round the room for the things I lose, and never finds them. It's a mystery, that's what it is. But you hurry up and find my glasses. They'll be round my chair somewhere.'

The twins looked, but they couldn't see any glasses anywhere. Old Grandad got rather cross.

'Children nowadays don't seem able to use their eyes,' he said. 'If only I could get out of this chair I'd find those glasses straight away! Feel under the carpet, boy. They must be some-where!'

But they weren't. The twins stood up, looking hot and untidy, for they had been all over the floor. Old Grandad was quite disgusted with them.

'You wait till Annie comes back,' he said. 'She'll see them. You don't know how to look.'

Sally stared at him. She had looked very hard indeed! It wasn't fair to say things like that. She pulled at the rug on Old Grandad's knees.

'Perhaps they're caught in the rug,' she said. 'Or maybe you're sitting on your glasses!'

'Now, now, don't you suppose I've shaken out the rug and felt the seat of the chair?' said Old Grandad.

Then Simon remembered something. At home there was an old chair like this one, and once when he and Sally had sat in it, they had slid their hands down the sides of it, and you'd never believe the things they had found there! Perhaps Old Grandad's glasses had slipped down into the sides of *his* chair! Simon slid his hand down the right-hand side, and his fingers felt something at once. He pulled out his hand, and found that he was holding a pencil!

'Here's your pencil, anyway!' he said, and

Old Grandad took it in delight. Then Sally put her hand down and brought up a big white hanky, neatly folded.

'So *that's* where my clean hanky went to!' said Old Grandad. 'Whatever next?'

Well, you really wouldn't believe the things the twins found down the sides of Old Grandad's chair. There were two playing-cards, a fine pen-knife, a small book, a pipe, a pair of scissors, a sixpence, a penny and a shilling – and the lost glasses as well!

Old Grandad kept shouting in surprise each time the twins brought up something. Then he began to laugh, and when Mrs Straws came back with the eggs, they were all three roaring with laughter. It was really too funny to think of Old Grandad solemnly sitting in a chair where he had lost so many things!

'Oh!' said Mrs Straws, when she saw all the different things. 'Wherever did they come from? You don't mean to say you stuffed them down the sides of your chair?'

'No, Annie, no, they must have slipped down,' said Old Grandad, chuckling. 'Here are your scissors, and your little book. And here you are twins, a shilling, sixpence and a penny – they're yours!'

'Oh no. *We* didn't put them down there,' said Sally.

'No, but you pulled them out, and you deserve them for being so clever,' said Old Grandad. 'You buy something nice, and next time you come for eggs you can feel down the sides of my old chair again!'

The lost tortoise

DANIEL and Rebecca had a tortoise of their very own. It was the only pet they had, for Mummy would not have a kitten or a puppy. They took it in turns to polish his shell for him every week. Mummy lent them a tiny pot of polish and a cloth and you should have seen Archibald the tortoise when he had been freshly polished!

'He could see his own face in his shell if he could get his head out far enough!' laughed Daniel.

The two children collected rose petals for Archibald to eat, because he liked them so much. He crunched up the petals in his funny little mouth, and then looked round for more. Once a week Rebecca gave him a feast of hard-boiled egg, and when he saw her coming with this in a little saucer he almost stood up on his hind legs with joy.

Archibald became very tame indeed. He always stretched out his neck to be scratched gently underneath when he saw Daniel or Rebecca. He made little hissing noises to tell them that he loved them. He was a very happy tortoise.

He had only a small garden to live in but he was very pleased with it. There was a little piece of green grass that ran right down to the fence. And, on each side of the grass, were small, narrow beds where Daddy grew a few flowers. That was all the garden there was. Archibald could not possibly wander away, for there was a fence all round, so he was quite safe.

All through the summer he lived a happy life. Daniel and Rebecca played with him whenever they were home from school, and he always looked out for them. Mummy said he was the tamest tortoise she had ever known.

The summer days passed. Autumn came. A few leaves blew down into the little garden, and Archibald tasted them. But he didn't like them, so he pulled at the dewy green grass.

He was cold at night. He tried to huddle under a bush, but one night the frost found him there and nipped his nose, though he had it well hidden under his shell

Daniel and Rebecca wondered why Archibald seemed so miserable. And then, what do you think happened? He disappeared! Yes, one morning when Daniel and Rebecca ran home from school, and Rebecca got a little dish of hard-boiled egg for him, she couldn't find him.

'Archibald! Archibald! Archibald!' she called. But no Archibald came.

'Mummy, have you seen Archibald?' Rebecca asked, running indoors. But Mummy hadn't noticed him at all that morning. Daniel came out to help Rebecca to look.

The two children hunted all over the garden for Archibald. He wasn't on the grass. He wasn't under any bush. He wasn't by the fence. He had completely disappeared.

Daniel and Rebecca were very upset. Rebecca began to cry.

'He's our only pet,' she sobbed. 'And I was so fond of him. Now he's gone!'

'Someone must have stolen him,' said Daniel. 'Oh, Mummy, isn't it a shame?'

When Daddy came home that afternoon he was surprised to see two such miserable faces. 'Whatever is the matter?' he said. 'Have you gone to the bottom of the class? Or lost all your money?'

'No,' said Daniel. 'We've lost old Archibald, Daddy. He's disappeared.'

'Nonsense!' said Daddy. 'He couldn't possibly have escaped from the garden, because of the fence all round. He must be there somewhere.'

Daddy went out to look. He hunted everywhere – and suddenly his sharp eyes caught sight of a little hump in the bed at the right side of the garden. 'What's this I wonder?' said Daddy, and he scraped away at the earth.

Well, it was Archibald! He had buried himself deep down in the earth, so it was no wonder that the children couldn't see him. Daddy gently pulled him up and brushed the earth off him.

'But Daddy, why ever did he hide himself away like that?' asked Daniel, astonished. 'He hasn't dug himself into the earth before.'

'Ah,' said Daddy, 'you don't know the way of tortoises yet, Danny! When the weather is frosty a tortoise feels very cold, for his real home is in far-off hot countries. So, to get away from the cold, he digs down into the earth and buries himself. Then the frost cannot get him and kill him. He was being very sensible indeed.'

'But, Daddy, if he does that, you might perhaps dig him up when you dig the garden,' said Rebecca, brushing the tortoise's shell clean. 'You might break his lovely shell!'

'Yes, so I might,' said Daddy. 'Well, we'll find him a box, Becky, and put some earth at the bottom. Then we'll cover him with a cloth, and put him in the bicycle shed, on a shelf.'

'But the shed is cold,' said Daniel. 'Can't we put him in the warm cupboard under the stairs, Daddy?'

'No,' said Daddy, 'because if a tortoise is too warm in the winter, he won't sleep properly. If we put him in the shed, the frost will not get him, and yet he will be cold enough to sleep until the spring comes again.'

So they found a box for sleepy old Archibald, put him in it, and covered him up. Daddy put him on the shelf in the shed, and there he is now, fast asleep until the spring.

The scarecrow

Simon and Sally often went for a walk in the fields near their home. There was one walk they liked very much because there were four stiles to climb over, and a little swing gate to go through.

One day the farmer planted seeds in one of his fields. The birds came and pecked them up, so he put an old scarecrow in the middle of the field to scare them away.

Simon and Sally suddenly saw the scarecrow as they were climbing over the stile to go into the field.

'What's that?' said Sally, frightened.

'A scarecrow,' said Simon. 'I don't like him, do you?'

'No. I can't bear him,' said Sally. 'He frightens me. He's so ugly.'

The scarecrow was indeed very ugly. His head was a turnip stuck on a pole. The farmer had cut eyes, nose and mouth out of the turnip head. He had a very old hat on, and the coat he wore had once belonged to the farmer, and was dirty and full of holes.

He wore a ragged pair of trousers that flapped wildly whenever the wind blew. His arms were sticks that stuck straight out.

He stared at the two children with his turnip eyes. 'I don't like him,' said Sally. 'I know he's not alive, but really he almost looks as if he'll walk across the field right up to the stile.'

'Don't be silly,' said Simon. But he didn't like the look of the scarecrow either. The wind blew and the scarecrow's clothes flapped hard, scaring all the rooks away at once.

'Let's go another way,' said Simon, and he climbed back over the stile. 'We won't come this way any more. Do you think we're cowards, Sally?'

'Yes. I suppose we are,' said Sally. 'It's a pity because this is our very nicest walk. It's such fun to go to the farm this way – and it takes ages the other way round.'

Still, they didn't think they would walk

through the scarecrow's field again, even if it made them feel like cowards. Sally knew she was silly, but she couldn't help feeling that the scarecrow might chase her.

The ugly old scarecrow came into their dreams that night. Sally screamed and Mummy came to see what was the matter.

'I dreamt that the scarecrow was running after me,' sobbed Sally. 'I'm afraid of him.'

'What's the matter with him, poor old scarecrow?' said Mummy. 'Out there in the wind and the rain all alone, with no one to say hallo – and the children running away from him.'

All the same, whatever Mummy said, Sally still didn't feel much better. So the very next day Mummy went to take a look at the old scarecrow herself. How she laughed when she saw the old turnip-head man flapping his clothes at the birds and scaring them away. She saw something else too, and she stood and looked for a long time.

On Saturday she said to Sally and Simon, 'I'm going to take you for a walk. Get your things on.'

They put on their coats, and went with Mummy. She took them to the field where the scarecrow stood, his hat all crooked on his turnip head.

'Oh! We don't want to go through this field,' said Sally in alarm.

'But I want to show you a rabbit's home, and a robin's nest, with three eggs in it,' said Mummy. The twins stared at her in delight.

'A robin's nest, with eggs in! Oh, we haven't seen one this year!' said Simon.

'Show me,' said Sally, and took hold of Mummy's hand very tightly. Mummy went over the stile and the two children followed.

Mummy didn't follow the path round the edge of the field. She walked carefully over the field itself right up to the scarecrow! The twins hung behind, not liking this at all.

'You said you'd show us a robin's nest and a rabbit's home,' said Simon. 'I can't see either of them.'

'No. The old scarecrow is guarding them well,' said Mummy. 'He's keeping them safe. He scares the rooks, but he likes the rabbits and the robins. Scarecrow, where do the rabbits live?'

The scarecrow stared at Mummy, and then one of his trouser-legs moved in the wind. Below it the children saw a rabbit-hole, and Sally felt sure she could see a pair of ears ready to pop out as soon as they were gone!

'Oh! This is where the rabbits live!' she cried. 'Where is the robin's nest, scarecrow?'

The scarecrow looked at them all, and Sally saw that his face wasn't really ugly, only queer, because it was made of turnip. He swung his coat in the wind, and Simon gave a cry of delight.

'Look! The nest is in his pocket! And there are three red-brown eggs there. Mummy, isn't that wonderful – a nest in a scarecrow's pocket?'

'Yes,' said Mummy. 'He must be glad that the bright-eyed robin likes him enough to build in his pocket, and that the rabbits trust him enough to make a hole by his feet so that they can pop in and out. It's a pity that children are afraid of him, isn't it?'

'I'm as brave as a robin any day!' said Simon,

and he actually patted the scarecrow on the shoulder. 'Scarecrow, we aren't afraid of you any more. If you are the robin's friend and the rabbit's, you're ours, too! We'll come and see you every day.'

Annabel's little thimble

ANNABEL had a lovely little work-basket that Granny had given her. In it were needles of all sizes, a bright pair of scissors, black, white, grey, green and blue cottons, and a pincushion. But best and brightest of all was Annabel's little silver thimble.

Mummy had given that to her on her birthday. It was made of real silver, so it shone and glittered brightly. It fitted Annabel's middle finger beautifully, and she was very proud of it.

She took great care to keep her work-basket shut when Rascal the jackdaw was about. He was a tame jackdaw that Daddy had picked up from the ground when he was a tiny bird, fallen from the nest. Daddy had fed him and tamed him and now he hopped and flew around the house, and loved to talk to anyone he met.

But he was so fond of bright things that everyone was careful not to leave any spoons, brooches, necklaces or silver pencils about. If they did, Rascal the jackdaw would take them and hide them away in one of his cubby-holes in the garden. Once Daddy had found a whole collection of things tucked away in a corner of the potting-shed – a pair of scissors, two spoons from next door, some pieces of silver paper and a little gilt pin!

Annabel had always been careful of her little thimble, because she had seen Rascal looking at it two or three times, when she put it on her finger. But there came a morning when she forgot.

She was sewing a new bonnet for her doll when Mummy called her. 'Quick, Annabel! There's Auntie Sue!'

Annabel hurriedly put down her work, stuck her thimble on top of it and ran to meet her aunt.

And as soon as she was safely out of the door, Rascal the jackdaw came in at the window. He spied the bright little thimble at once and pounced on it. Ah! He had wanted that for a long time. Where should he put it?

He went and sat on the kitchen window-sill, holding it in his beak. Mummy had been busy making Christmas puddings, but now she had left everything to go and greet Auntie Sue. Rascal sat and looked at all the bright things on the table beside the pudding bowl. There were six silver threepenny bits, four sixpences, a silver elephant, a tiny silver doll, a little silver horseshoe and one big, bright shilling. Mummy was going to put them in the Christmas pudding for luck. It was always fun at Christmas time to see who got the treasures out of the pudding.

Then Mummy came back and started to drop the shining things into the pudding. He thought she was hiding them. What a good place to hide them! He waited until she went to the cupboard to get something and then he hopped on to the table. He dropped Annabel's silver thimble into the sticky mixture and then covered it neatly up with the currants and chopped nuts in the dish. Ha! It was a splendid hiding-place!

But what a to-do there was when Annabel ran to get her sewing again! Where was her dear little silver thimble? Gone! Nowhere to be found at all! Everyone hunted all over the place, but it couldn't be found.

'Rascal must have taken it,' said Annabel in tears. So Daddy went to look in all the hidey-holes that he knew the jackdaw had. But they were empty. Not one of them had Annabel's thimble in it.

She was very unhappy. She did so like her thimble, and besides Mummy had given it to her. It was dreadful to lose something Mummy had bought for her. No other thimble would be half so nice.

'Perhaps someone will give you another one at Christmas time,' said Mummy.

'It won't be as nice as the one *you* gave me, Mummy,' said Annabel. 'It helped me to sew so nicely. I shan't sew so well with any other thimble, I'm sure.'

'Rubbish!' said Mummy smiling She made up her mind to ask Annabel's Auntie Sue to give the little girl another thimble for Christmas. Mummy wanted to give Annabel a new doll. Auntie Sue promised Mummy she would buy a lovely new thimble for Annabel.

But she forgot about it! Yes, she bought

Annabel a fairy-tale book instead, so when Christmas morning came there was no silver thimble for Annabel. She was so disappointed. But she didn't say anything, of course. She loved all her presents very much, especially her new doll, but she *would* have liked a new thimble!

Christmas dinner-time came. What a big turkey there was – and what a lot of people to eat it! Granny and Grandpa, three aunties, two uncles and Cousin Jane and Cousin Jimmy, as well as Annabel herself and Mummy and Daddy. But there was quite enough for everybody!

Then Mummy brought in the Christmas pudding with a bit of holly stuck on top. How excited the children were!

'Hope I get a silver threepenny bit!' cried Cousin Jane.

'Hope I get a sixpence!' cried Cousin Jimmy.

'And I hope I get the little silver elephant!' cried Annabel. Everyone was served, and then what a hunt there was through the pieces of pudding to see if anyone had been lucky.

'A threepenny bit for me!' cried Daddy.

'Sixpence for me!' cried Cousin Jimmy, fishing out a sixpence from his piece of pudding.

'What have *I* got?' cried Annabel, feeling her spoon scrape against something hard. She looked at the treasure *she* had, and then she cried out in astonishment.

'Mummy! Daddy! It's my own little silver thimble that I lost ages ago! Oh, look! How did it get in the pudding?'

Mummy and Daddy *were* surprised! Mummy said she hadn't put it in the pudding.

'I expect it's a little trick Santa Claus played on you!' she said.

'Caw, caw, caw!' suddenly said a loud voice, and Rascal the jackdaw looked in at the window.

'Oh, Rascal, I wonder if *you* took my thimble and dropped it into the pudding!' cried Annabel. 'Did you, Rascal?'

'Caw, caw, caw!' said the jackdaw. And Annabel didn't know whether he meant yes or no! But she didn't mind; she had got back her little silver thimble after all. It was the nicest Christmas surprise she could have had!

At Seaside Cottage

Part 1

IT was summer time. The sky was blue and the sun shone down. Peter was lying on the grass with Janet beside him.

'I'm so hot I'm sure I'm going to melt,' said Peter.

'We can't take off any more of our clothes,' said Janet. 'We've only got bathing costumes on as it is!'

'I wish we were by the sea,' said Peter, rolling over on his front. 'Oh, Janet, think of it! Little waves rolling up the beach, golden sand to dig in, lots of bathing, and perhaps a boat to go sailing in!'

'Woof!' said a voice suddenly, and there came the sound of scampering feet. Then a golden spaniel flung himself on the two children, barking madly.

'Oh, Scamper! Get off my middle,' cried

Janet. The dog at once jumped on to Peter, who squealed.

'Scamper! Stop licking my ear! Oh, what a wet tongue you've got. Stop kissing me, you silly dog! I shall have to get a towel in a minute!'

'Woof!' said Scamper, and licked Peter's nose instead.

Peter took hold of one of the spaniel's long ears. 'If you don't stop licking me, I won't let go your ear!' he said. 'What's made you so excited today?'

'He looks as if he has some good news for us, doesn't he?' said Janet. 'Scamper, tell us what it is!'

'Woof!' said Scamper, and shook his ear free. Then he galloped off up the garden. Peter sat up.

'What *is* the matter with him? Oh, there's Mummy. *She* looks pleased about something too. Hallo, Mummy!'

Mummy came down the garden with Scamper jumping up and down beside her. She was smiling.

'Well, children,' she said. 'I've got something

nice to tell you. We're all going for a holiday by the sea!'

'*Mummy!* We were just saying how we wished we were by the sea!' said Janet.

'And we *knew* Scamper wanted to tell us some good news!' said Peter. 'When are we going?'

'Tomorrow,' said Mummy. 'So you will have to come and help me to pack at once. Granny has invited us to stay with her in her cottage at Sandy Cove.'

'Oh!' cried the children in delight, and they got up and began to run round just as madly as Scamper.

'I love Granny's cottage. The sea comes almost to her back gate,' cried Peter.

'Scamper, you've never even *seen* the sea. You'll love it.'

'Woof!' said Scamper, quite agreeing.

They all set off to the house to pack, chattering at the tops of their voices.

'I shall take my ship.'

'I'm glad my doll has a bathing costume. She'll love to wear it.'

'Woof! Woof!'

'Don't let's forget to take some balls to play with on the sand.'

'Woof!'

'Oh, Mummy, isn't it lovely? I feel so excited!'

All the packing was done by the evening. Daddy came home with the train tickets, and even Scamper had a dog-ticket. He felt very proud.

Everyone was excited the next day. Janet said she couldn't possibly eat any breakfast, so Scamper ate her sausage because Mummy said it couldn't be left in the larder. Scamper thought that was a very good beginning to a holiday – a whole sausage at once!

'Here's the taxi, quick, it's at the door!' shouted Peter suddenly. The taximan went to help Daddy with the luggage. Soon it was all in the taxi.

Daddy went all round the house to make sure that every window was closed. Then he slammed the front door and got into the taxi with the others.

'We're off!' he said. 'No, Scamper, sit on the

floor, please. You really can't sit on my knee.'

'I hope we're in time for the train,' said Peter. 'Oh, Mummy, wouldn't it be awful if we didn't catch it!'

'We could get the next one, silly,' said Janet. 'Look – here we are at the station already. Mummy, there's a train in. Oh quick, in case it's ours!'

They all got out of the taxi, and at that very moment the train began to pull slowly out of the station.

'It's all right,' said Daddy, seeing the children's alarmed faces. 'That's not our train. It's going the wrong way!'

They went into the station. It was an exciting place. A goods train came in and the children counted the trucks behind it.

'It's got thirty-four trucks to pull!' cried Peter. 'The most we've ever counted! Oh, Mummy, hadn't I better put Scamper on the lead in case he gets on the line? He will keep going to the edge of the platform.'

'Look – the signal's set to show our train is coming!' cried Janet. 'I can just see it coming. Yes, it's our train!'

So it was. It came rushing into the station, and poor Scamper was so frightened that he tried to get under a pile of luggage and hide.

'He thinks it's some kind of great big dog coming to eat him,' said Janet. 'Come on, Scamper – get in!'

They all got into an empty compartment. The children knelt up at the windows on opposite sides. Scamper got under the seat. He was still frightened.

The train began to move very slowly, and the children shouted with joy. 'We're moving! We're off to the sea!'

'Look, we can see our back garden!' cried Janet. Scamper came from under the seat and jumped up by her to look. 'See, Scamper, there is the cat next door. Wave your paw to her!'

It was great fun going in the train. There was such a lot to see from the windows. There were fields of cows, winding rivers with bridges over them, lots of back gardens, some neat and tidy, some badly-kept and full of weeds. There were dark tunnels to go through, high bridges to go over, and stations to stop at. The children couldn't think how Daddy and Mummy could sit and read when there was so much to be seen from the windows.

'Soon be there now,' said Daddy, after a long time. 'Look out for the first sight of the sea, children. You will see it after the next station.'

And so they did! Janet gave a squeal that made everyone jump. 'Oh look! I can see the sea, like a blue line over there! Look, Scamper, that's the sea!'

'Woof!' said Scamper, looking at a cat on a wall. He didn't know in the least what the sea was like.

'Next station's ours,' said Daddy, beginning to collect the bags off the rack.

The train came to a full stop at the next station, and couldn't go any farther because the line ended there. The children tumbled out of the carriage excitedly. They were at the sea at last!

'There's Granny! And Grandpa! Granny, we're here!'

Granny hugged them all, and patted Scamper. 'Welcome to Sandy Cove!' she said. 'Let the porter bring the luggage. We can walk, it's so near.'

The sun shone down from a lovely blue sky. When the children turned the first corner they cried out in delight.

'The sea! Oh, look at all the sparkles on it. Grandpa, is the tide in or out?'

'Going out,' said Grandpa. 'You'll be able to dig in the sand all afternoon. Well, well, it's nice to have you here. Now I shall be able to have somebody to take me out on the big steamer. Granny won't come with me, because she's afraid of being sick!'

'*We'll* come, Grandpa! We'd love to,' said the children, and Scamper ran round and round them, getting in everyone's way, he was so excited.

'Oh, can we go down on the sands now, this very minute?' asked Janet. 'They do look so lovely.'

'Wait till after dinner,' said Granny. 'I'm sure you must be very hungry. I've got a nice lunch waiting for you.'

'What is it?' said Janet, suddenly feeling hungry.

'Cold meat, salad, and potatoes in their jackets,' said Granny.

'And lots of ice cream for a pudding,' added Grandpa.

'Our very favourite dinner!' said Peter, and he rushed on ahead to Granny's little cottage.

It was a pretty one, set right by the sea. The back garden ran down to the beach, and a little white gate led on to the sands.

'Has the sea ever come into your back garden?' asked Janet.

'Oh, yes. It often does in the winter,' said Granny, pushing open her little front gate. 'Now, welcome to Seaside Cottage, all of you. I hope you will have a lovely time here.'

'We shall, we shall!' said Peter, and gave her such a hug that he almost lifted her off her feet.

Soon they were all sitting down to dinner. How hungry they were! 'I've got my seaside appetite already,' said Peter. 'I could eat my dinner all over again!'

'You can't possibly eat any more, Peter,' said Mummy. 'Now, go up to your room, both of you, and get into your shorts and sandals. Then you can go straight out on to the beach.'

It wasn't long before Peter, Janet and Scamper were running down Granny's back garden, through the little white gate, and out on to the yellow sands. They all danced about like mad things. 'We're at the seaside! Our holiday's only just beginning! Hurrah, hurrah, hurrah!'

'Woof, woof, woof!' barked Scamper at the top of his voice.

'Come down to the water and see the sea, Scamper,' said Janet. 'Come along. We'll run right down to the very edge.'

So off they all went, but when Scamper really saw the sea, stretching away blue and smooth for miles and miles, he was frightened. And when a wave ran up and caught his paw, he barked in fright.

'It's all right, Scamper. The sea won't eat you,' cried Peter. 'Come on, let's paddle.'

And in went the two children, their toes loving the feel of the warm water and soft sand. They paddled till the water came above their knees. The little waves splashed round them, and soon Scamper forgot to be afraid and came bounding in the sea after them.

'Oh, Scamper! You'll have to swim if you come out much deeper,' cried Peter. 'And we none of us have learnt to swim yet.'

'Oh, look! Scamper can swim! He's swimming beautifully. Look how he uses all his legs at once!' called Janet. 'Peter, how does he know how to swim? He hasn't had a single lesson.'

'Dogs don't need to be taught,' said Grandpa's voice, from the edge of the sea. 'But children do. You must learn while you are here, and as soon as you can both swim six strokes we'll go on the steamer!'

What fun the children had that first day! They dug a big castle, with Grandpa helping. They made a wide moat round it for the sea to fill. They decorated it with seaweed and shells. They went to buy a little flag to put on the top. It did look a lovely castle.

'Sit on it with Scamper, Janet,' said Peter. 'Let the tide come right up.'

'It won't be up till after tea,' said Grandpa. 'Look, here comes Mummy with a picnic tea.'

Tea was lovely. They all had it sitting on the sands. Scamper upset Janet's milk, and ate Granny's bun when she wasn't looking, but otherwise he was a very good dog.

'Now the tide's coming up, look,' said Grandpa. 'Go and sit on the castle with Scamper, Janet.'

So off they went, and soon Janet was proudly sitting on the very top, waving the little Union Jack, while Scamper growled fiercely every time a wave came too near. When one actually dared to touch the castle he barked very angrily indeed. 'Woof, woof! Woof, woof!'

A big wave came up and washed right round

the castle. Janet gave a squeal. 'Oh, the castle is going. I felt it!'

Another wave came. Scamper barked so furiously that Granny felt quite alarmed. Then a still bigger wave came, and Janet had to stand up in case she was washed away with the castle!

'That was fun!' she said, wading back to shore. 'Come on, Scamper. Good dog! I'm sure you must have made the waves feel very frightened.'

It was lovely going to bed in the little room under the roof, at Granny's cottage.

'I like this ceiling, don't you, Janet?' said Peter. 'It's not straight like ours at home. It comes slanting down almost to the floor. Oh, I do like being here!'

At Seaside Cottage

Part 2

It was lovely waking up the next morning. The children could hear the sound of the sea, and they could hear the seagulls calling.

'It sounds as if they're laughing,' said Janet, jumping out of bed and going to the window. 'Get up, Peter. The sea is as blue as cornflowers!'

Grandpa gave them their first swimming lesson that day. He was very good and patient with them. He had to be quite stern with Peter, though, because he was afraid that Grandpa would let go his hold of him and drop him under the water

'Now don't be silly! You can trust me when I say I shan't let you go under the water. Watch Janet! She is much better than you are, and you are seven, a whole year older!'

Then Peter went red, and tried harder.

'Very good,' said Grandpa 'You are doing the arm strokes better now. My word, you'll soon be able to swim after all. Then we'll go on the steamer.'

Daddy made them run about and play ball on the sands after they had bathed, to get them nice and warm. Scamper loved that. He always fetched the ball when it ran into the water.

But sometimes he didn't want to give it back to the others. He would run off down the beach with the ball, and make the children chase him for miles.

The weather was so lovely that they had all their meals, except breakfast, out of doors. The children got brown after two days in the sun, and they ate so much that Granny really thought she had better give them five meals a day!

'Let's go shrimping this evening,' said Grandpa, and he went out and bought three shrimping nets. Then they went shrimping in the shallow sandy edge of the sea.

'I've got five at once!' cried Janet in delight.

'And I've got eight!' called Peter. 'Grandpa, did you catch any that time?'

'Only two,' said Grandpa. 'We shall soon get our baskets full!'

Granny cooked the shrimps for supper. The children ate them with brown bread and butter. They were delicious.

'I do want to go and explore the rock pools,' said Janet, one day. 'Can we, Granny?'

'Of course. But go at low tide, dear, because they get very deep at high tide,' she said.

So Peter and Janet went to the blue pools

that lay between the seaweedy rocks. Peter took his boat to sail on one pool. 'Look!' he called to Janet. 'She sails beautifully!'

They climbed about all over the rocks when they had sailed Peter's boat. And suddenly Janet slipped on the seaweed!

'Help!' she cried.

But before Peter could turn round, she had slid backwards into a deep pool. Splash! In she went, and the water went right over her head as she sat down in the pool.

Peter dragged her up, gasping and choking. She began to cry.

'Don't cry,' said Peter. 'Let's go back and tell Mummy all about it.'

He took Janet back to Mummy. Daddy laughed when Janet told him what had happened. And then Janet began to laugh too.

'I expect I looked funny,' she said.

Then suddenly Peter looked alarmed. 'My boat! We left it on the pond! Oh, I do hope nobody has taken it. I wonder if I shall know which pool it is.'

He ran off to get his boat. But soon he was back, looking very upset. 'I can't find my boat. It's gone. Somebody must have taken it.'

'Look! What's Scamper got?' said Mummy suddenly. They all looked round. Scamper was trotting towards them from the rock pools, and in his mouth he had Peter's boat!

'Oh, you clever dog!' cried Peter in delight. 'You found it for me. Scamper, you're the best dog in the world. Can I buy him an ice-cream, Mummy? He does so love them.'

So Scamper had an ice-cream all to himself.

Another day, Grandpa gave Daddy and the two children a great treat. He paid Jock the fisherman to take them out in his fishing-boat to fish!

Jock's boat had a sail. It was a red one and looked lovely against the blue sky. Jock took down his sail and threw out the anchor when they were far enough out.

'Now here's where we'll get plenty of fish,' he said. 'Here's a line for you, Peter, and one for you, Janet.'

Janet caught two fish, and Peter caught three. Grandpa caught six, and Jock caught eight.

'A very fine afternoon's work,' said Jock with a grin that showed all his white teeth. 'Now, up with the sail and we'll be off back to the shore. You'll have some nice fried fish for your supper tonight!'

The wind filled the red sail, and the boat sped back to Sandy Cove. Janet and Peter each had a turn at the tiller. They felt very grand to be able to hold the little boat on her course.

'When I'm grown up I shall have a boat just like this for my own,' said Peter.

'What will you call her?' asked Janet 'Jock's boat is called *Saucy Sue*.'

'Then I'll call mine *Cheeky Janet*, after you,' said Peter, and that made everyone laugh.

As they came near the shore Peter saw the high cliffs farther along the cove.

'Are there any caves there?' he asked Jock.

'What? Along there in those cliffs?' said Jock. 'Oh yes. Plenty of them. You should go and explore them, but mind you do it when the tide's out or you'll get caught inside. The water comes right up to them round along there.'

'Oh Daddy – can Janet and I go and explore the caves tomorrow?' asked Peter. 'Do say yes!

We might find some smugglers' caves. Mightn't we, Jock?'

'Well, there's no knowing,' said Jock, his bright blue eyes twinkling at them. 'They do say there were smugglers here a hundred years ago.'

The very next day Peter and Janet set off to explore the caves. They took Scamper with them, of course, and he raced along beside them, barking at any gull that dared to come and walk on the beach.

It was quite a long way round the cove to the cliffs where the caves were. The first cave was small and low. The next one was bigger but it didn't go very far into the cliff. But the next cave looked a likely one. It ran right back into the cliff and had a very sandy floor, clean and smooth. Peter had brought his torch with him and he switched it on.

'Look, Janet! There's an archway here at the back of this cave, and I do believe it goes right back into another cave. Let's go, shall we?'

So they went through the archway and came into another cave, very dark and seaweedy.

'Let's play here,' said Peter. 'We could be smugglers!'

Scamper dashed in and out excitedly, dragging a long bit of seaweed behind him. The children explored the second cave and then, to their great delight, they found that rough steps in the back cave led upwards into a third cave.

'This *is* exciting!' cried Peter, climbing up, his torch throwing a bright light before him.

The third cave was small and rather smelly. The children explored it thoroughly, but they could not find anything there that they thought had anything to do with smugglers.

'We've been here a long time,' said Janet. 'And do listen to Scamper barking down there in the other cave. What's the matter with him?'

They soon knew! The tide had come right up to the first cave and was splashing inside. They were caught. They stood staring out at the great, heaving stretch of blue sea, full of dismay.

'*Now* what shall we do?' said Peter.

Suddenly Scamper splashed into the waves and swam off valiantly. 'I do believe he's gone to fetch help,' said Janet, almost crying. 'Oh, I do hope he has!'

Scamper had. He swam right round the cliffs till he came to the sandy beach. Then he bounded along to Seaside Cottage. He barked and barked, and tried to drag Daddy out of the door.

'The children are in danger!' said Mummy suddenly. 'That's what Scamper has come to say. They've gone to those caves and been caught by the tide. Oh dear!'

'Now don't worry, my dear. I'll get Jock's boat and he and I will go and get the children,' said Daddy. So off he went and very soon he, Jock and Scamper were rowing round the cliffs to the cave where the children stood, alone and frightened. Scamper barked to them.

Daddy and Jock got the children into the boat. Scamper licked them madly. He was so pleased to have saved them. Janet hugged him.

'Darling Scamper! Daddy, isn't he wonderful? He knew we were in danger and he fetched you.'

Daddy had a few words to say about foolish children who didn't remember the tides. 'And you especially, Peter, ought to have been more careful,' he said, 'because a brother must always look after his sister. I don't feel very pleased with you.'

But everyone was pleased with Scamper, and you should have seen the dinner Granny put down for him that night.

At Seaside Cottage

Part 3

BEFORE two weeks had gone by Peter and Janet could both swim six strokes. Grandpa was very proud of them both.

'Now, I must keep my word and let you take me on the steamer,' he said. 'Shall we go this afternoon?'

'Oh yes!' cried the children. So that afternoon they walked to the little pier where small red steamers came six times a day.

'There comes the steamer now!' cried Peter in excitement. 'Look, Grandpa. It's puffing away like anything. Will it turn round at the pier?'

'She will turn before she arrives at the pier,' said Grandpa, 'and back up against it, till she's sideways on.'

They got their tickets and went to wait for the little red steamer. Before they could get on, a lot of people got off. Then Grandpa, Peter and Janet all went on board with the other people who were waiting.

'Oh, it's a lovely steamer!' cried Peter, exploring every corner. 'Look, Janet, you can even go downstairs in it.'

'Yes, that goes down to the cabin,' said Grandpa. 'In case it rains, you know. But it won't rain, so we'll sit up here on deck. Come along.'

What fun it was when the steamer started off. It gave a deep hoot that made the children jump, and then set off quite fast over the sea.

'It's going to Pride Bay!' said Peter. 'That's a big place, isn't it, Grandpa? Is it as nice as Sandy Cove?'

'Well, you'll see,' said Grandpa. 'Now look how small our little pier is. We've come quite a long way already.'

'It's very windy, isn't it?' said Janet.

'Oh, isn't the sea blue? Look, Grandpa, is that Pride Bay far away over there? It looks so very small.'

But it didn't look small when they got to it. It

was a big seaside town. The beach was so crowded with people that the children could hardly see any sand. There was a lot of noise, too, bands playing, men shouting and children yelling.

'I don't like this,' said Janet. 'It's too big and noisy, and isn't the beach dirty? I like Sandy Cove best, Grandpa. Shall we just have an ice-cream somewhere and catch the next steamer back? It's the steamer-ride I like, not the place we've come to!'

'That's just what *I* feel!' said Grandpa, looking quite pleased. 'Sandy Cove for me every time. Look, we'll go and get an ice-cream over there, up on the cliff, and we can watch for the next steamer to come.'

So they had an ice-cream up on the cliff, where it was windy and fresh. Pride Bay was a beautiful bay, blue and calm. It was fun to watch the little red steamer they had come on, go puffing away, and another one come to meet it from somewhere up the coast.

They went down to the crowded beach to get to the pier. Pierrots were playing and singing

77

to the people. Ice-cream men did a fine trade.
A string of little donkeys stood patiently waiting for riders.

'Let's have just one ride!' said Peter.

So they had a ride, and even Grandpa did
too. The three donkeys galloped along the sands
and back again. Then it was time to go to the
pier to wait for the little red steamer.

It was lovely to arrive back at Sandy Cove
again. Granny, Mummy, Daddy and Scamper
were at the little pier to meet them. Scamper
flung himself at them as if he hadn't seen them
for a whole year!

'It was a lovely trip,' said Janet, 'but we *are*
glad to come back to Sandy Cove. It's the
nicest seaside place there is!'

'It's a pity we've ever got to leave it,' said
Peter. 'Oh Mummy, is our holiday soon coming
to an end? I shall be so sad if it is.'

'I'm afraid it is,' said Mummy. 'We must go
the day after tomorrow.'

'Oh dear! Not so soon as that!' cried Janet.
'Oh Mummy, we must collect heaps of shells,
and some ribbon seaweed too, to take back –
and can we take some crabs?'

'Oh no,' said Mummy. 'Not crabs. They wouldn't live away from the sea. But you can hunt for shells and take some nice seaweed back, if you like.'

'Only one more whole day,' said Janet, as they got into bed that night. 'Isn't it sad, Peter? Why do lovely holidays like this go so quickly?'

'We must do simply *everything* tomorrow,' said Peter. 'We must dig, and paddle, and bathe, and shrimp, and go out in Jock's boat. It's the last chance we'll have!'

So on that last day the two children were very busy. They dug an enormous castle with a moat that ran down to the sea.

They paddled with Scamper and they bathed with him. Janet swam eight strokes and Peter swam nine.

They went out in Jock's boat for an hour and saw him take up some of his lobster pots with lobsters in them.

They went to the rock pools and sailed Peter's boat – but this time they brought it safely back with them!

They got their fishing nets and shrimped

when the tide was low, and they caught more shrimps than ever before. They found a box for shells and filled it. And they both found a beautiful long piece of ribbon seaweed to take home and hang up to tell the weather.

'When it's dry you'll know the weather will be fine. When it's wet, the weather will be rainy or cloudy,' said Granny.

*

At last the time came to go. Granny and Grandpa went to see them off in the train. Scamper was sad too, and he put his tail right down.

'I don't like letting you go,' said Granny. 'I really don't. I don't know what I shall do without you all.'

'I shall only let them go if they promise me something,' said Grandpa suddenly.

'What?' asked the children.

'Promise me you'll come back next year in the summer holidays,' said Grandpa. 'Do you promise?'

'Oh *yes*, of *course* we promise!' cried the children, as the guard waved his flag.

'We'll come back next year. Good-bye, Granny; good-bye, Grandpa; good-bye, Sandy Cove!'

Granny's kittens

'JANE, put on your coat and go to Granny's,' said Mummy. 'She has some home-made sweets for my sale of work, and I told her you would fetch them.'

'Oh, yes, Mummy. I'll go now,' said Jane, pleased. 'Granny's cat has got kittens, you know, and I shall see them, if she hasn't given them all away yet. Oh, Mummy, I do so wish we could have one.'

But Mummy didn't like cats, and she shook her head. 'No, dear. Don't keep asking me that. Now, hurry up and go.'

Jane soon got to Granny's, and the first thing she did was to ask about the kittens.

'They've all gone but one, the prettiest of the lot,' said Granny. 'It's the little white one. Now, where is the little monkey? Call it.'

'Kitty, kitty, kitty!' called Jane, but the kitten didn't come. Jane looked everywhere for it. She looked under the bed, under the couch, and out in the garden. Only Tabby, the big mother cat, was there, sitting washing herself on the wall.

'Where's your white kitten?' asked Jane, but Tabby took no notice. Jane thought her kittens were much nicer than she was. Tabby never played at all.

'I can't find the kitten, Granny,' said Jane, sadly. 'I'm sorry I can't, because I'm sure next time I come it will be gone.'

'What a pity,' said Granny. 'It's always hiding away somewhere. Now, you had better go back, darling, because it is getting late.'

'What about the home-made sweets for Mummy's sale, Granny?' asked Jane. 'She said I was to bring them back.'

'Oh, yes,' said Granny. 'I've got everything ready in this basket. I've put the boxes of sweets at the very bottom, and above them I have put some knitted gloves and hot-water bottle covers I have made for the sale, too. The basket is quite light, so you can easily carry it.'

Jane picked it up. She kissed Granny good-bye, and went down the path. Granny had given her one of her bits of home-made toffee, and Jane sucked it as she went.

The basket was quite heavy. It dragged at Jane's arm, and she took it in the other hand. 'Dear me,' she said, 'it feels heavy, though Granny said it was light. I *shall* be tired when I get home!'

When she got home, she put the basket on the table. 'I'll unpack it for you,' said Jane, and she lifted off two hot-water bottle covers, beautifully knitted by Granny. And then Jane got such a surprise!

The little white kitten lay curled up in the basket, settled cosily on the knitted gloves! It had crept in there when it felt tired, and had gone fast asleep. It opened big, wondering eyes and stood up to stretch itself.

'Oh, Mummy! I brought the kitten home and I didn't know it!' cried Jane. 'Oh, isn't it sweet?'

The kitten leapt lightly on to the table. It rubbed its soft little head against Mummy's hand.

'Mummy, it likes you!' cried Jane. 'Oh, Mummy, please, *please* let me keep it!'

'Miaow,' said the kitten, and rubbed its head against Mummy's hand again. She simply couldn't help stroking it.

'Yes. You can have it,' she said. 'It's too sweet for words. I don't like cats, but I've lost my heart to this kitten. I'll ring up Granny and tell her we'll keep it if she'll let us.'

'Oh, *thank* you!' said Jane. 'No wonder the basket felt heavy. You're mine, Kitty. How will you like that?'

'Miaow-ee-ow-ee-ow,' said the kitten. And you can guess what *that* meant!

Bluebell Wood

A BIG dog lived next door to the twins, Simon and Sally He was black and brown and had such a stump of a tail that it was hardly big enough to wag.

'He's a silly dog,' said Sally. 'He doesn't know any tricks, and he won't run after a stick or a ball.'

'He can't even sit up and beg when I show him a biscuit,' said Simon. 'I've tried to make him, but he just falls over every time.'

'And he still hasn't learnt not to walk on the flower-beds,' said Sally. 'He came in yesterday and walked all over ours. I think he's a stupid dog.'

'He's old,' said Mummy. 'He can't be bothered to learn tricks now. He should have been taught long ago not to walk on flower-beds and to chase a ball. He'll never learn now. But he's a nice friendly dog.'

'He's dull,' said Simon. 'He won't play, he won't run.'

'The only thing he does is to go out looking for rabbits,' said Sally. 'But he never catches one, and I'm sure that if a rabbit chased him he would run away!'

Mummy laughed. 'Well, don't bother with old Billy if you think he's silly and won't play. I'm quite sure he doesn't want to bother himself with *you*!'

So they didn't bother with Billy any more. They didn't call to him to go with them when they went for a walk. They didn't bounce a ball for him or throw him a stick. And Billy didn't take any notice of them either. He just lay in his front garden, or trotted off to look for rabbits in the woods, and didn't even wag his stump of a tail when the twins came by.

One day the twins went off to the woods to pick bluebells. Mummy had said she wanted some because they looked so lovely.

The woods were full of bluebells. They lay like blue pools between the trees, and there were so many that not even when each twin had picked more than a hundred did the bluebells seem any less.

'We could pick a million and they wouldn't be missed!' said Sally. 'Oh Simon, aren't they lovely? They look like patches of blue sky fallen down in the woods.'

The twins wandered on and on. Simon wanted to find a white bluebell because it was lucky, so they looked everywhere.

'It must be getting late,' said Sally, at last. 'I don't know the time, but my tummy tells me it's nearly dinner-time. I'm very, very hungry.'

'Well, let's go home then,' said Simon, and he turned down a path. 'Come on. I'm hungry too.'

But they hadn't gone very far before Simon stopped. 'This isn't right,' he said in alarm. 'I don't know this path!'

'Oh dear! We aren't lost, are we?' said Sally. 'I don't want to be lost.'

But they *were* lost. They went down this path and that path, but always they came to the end and found themselves even deeper in the wood. 'These paths are just rabbit-paths,' said Simon at last. 'They only lead to rabbit-holes.'

'Simon, shall we be like the babes in the wood and have to go to sleep and be covered up with leaves?' asked Sally. 'Oh, do find the right way.'

But Simon couldn't, and soon the twins stood under the big trees, with Sally crying and Simon looking very scared.

'Listen! There's a noise!' said Simon, suddenly.

'It's not a nice noise,' said Sally, tears falling down her cheeks. 'It's a nasty snuffly noise. It sounds like a big animal. Let's hide.'

But before they could hide, the big animal came round a bush, nose to ground, snuffling loudly as he went. And will you believe it – it was Billy! There he was, standing in front of the children, just as surprised to see them as they were to see him.

Sally flung herself on him. 'Billy! Oh, I'm so glad to see you! Are you lost too? Stay with us and guard us, Billy.'

Billy saw that Sally was unhappy. He licked her face with his big tongue. Simon took hold of his collar. 'Don't you run away and leave us,' he said. 'Let's all be lost together. Then when

people come to look for you and for us, they'll find us all.'

Billy pulled away from Simon. He didn't like to be held by his collar. He got himself free and trotted away. Simon ran after him.

'Don't go, don't go!' he cried.

Billy stopped, but he trotted on again as soon as Simon came up to him. Then when he was some way in front he stopped once more and looked around. His stump of a tail wagged itself. The twins ran to him, but again he trotted away in front. He wouldn't let them catch him. It was most annoying.

'He's so *silly*!' said Sally. 'He just won't understand that we want him with us. I feel safe with him.'

'He'll lead us deeper into the wood,' said Simon. 'We'll get more lost than ever. But we'd better follow him, Sally, because I feel safe when he's near, too.'

So they followed Billy, and when they got left behind he stopped and waited for them. Then on he went again. Right through the wood they went and at last they came out into a field. Across the field went Billy, and under a gate.

'Oh dear. Wherever is he taking us now?' said Simon. 'We must be miles away from home.'

And then, when they had climbed over the gate into a lane, Sally gave a shout. 'Simon! Simon! This is the lane that leads to our back garden! It is, it is! We're nearly home!'

So they were! They just had to run up the lane, and go into the gate at the end of their garden and race up to the house.

'You *are* late!' said Mummy, meeting them at the door. 'I was getting worried. I thought you were lost.'

'We were,' said Simon. 'But Billy was in the woods and he brought us all the way home. Fancy, Mummy, he knew the way quite well, though we didn't. And he was very kind. He kept waiting for us to catch up with him.'

'He's very clever,' said Sally. 'Much cleverer than we are. *He* wasn't lost at all.'

'I thought you said he was so silly,' said Mummy.

'We made a mistake,' said Simon. '*We* were the silly ones! Billy is old and wise. I shall go to the butcher's and buy him a bone this afternoon.'

The twins bought a big bone for Billy and took it to him. He was surprised and pleased. He wagged his stump of a tail and gave a little bark.

'He's saying thank you,' said Simon. 'Billy, we think you're clever, not silly at all. Please will you take us for a walk next time you go to the woods?'

'Woof,' said Billy, just as if he understood. And do you know, the very next day when he wanted to go and look for rabbits, he went to fetch the twins, so that they could go with him!

Rusty and the basket

EVERY day Gillian went down to the farm to fetch the eggs, and Rusty, her dog, went with her. They took a basket with them; Rusty carried it there, and Gillian carried it back. Rusty was very proud when he took the handle into his mouth and trotted off beside Gillian.

Once Gillian bumped into the gate when she opened it coming home and one of the eggs broke. It ran all over the bottom of the basket, and Rusty sniffed at it and thought how funny it smelt. After that, even when the egg dried up, the basket always smelt a bit eggy to Rusty.

Now one day Gillian's Mummy said to her, 'Will you go shopping for me today? I am going to be very busy in the garden, and it would be a help if you could go and get the butter from the dairy, and ask for my shoes at the cobbler's, and fetch my brooch from the jeweller's, if it is mended.'

'Oh, yes, Mummy, I'd love to do that!' said Gillian, joyfully. 'That will be a treat for me, because I don't usually go shopping by myself.'

'Well, here is a purse full of money,' said Mummy, and she put it at the bottom of the basket. 'Take care of it. And here are two letters to post. Take Rusty with you, if you like.'

'Rusty! Rusty!' called Gillian. But Rusty didn't come. He had gone for a walk by himself, just to see how many different smells he could find. So Gillian set off alone, and went up the lane to the farm. It was fun to go shopping!

She posted the letters. She came to the dairy and bought the butter. It was big and yellow in its packet, and smelt of milk. Gillian opened the purse and paid for it.

Then she went to the cobbler's and asked if Mummy's shoes were ready.

'Quite ready,' said the cobbler, and he took off his glasses to look along his shelves of mended shoes. He found Mummy's shoes, and put them in a brown paper bag. 'That will be four shillings and sixpence,' he said.

So Gillian opened the purse again and took out two half-crowns. She had some change. Do you know how much? Yes, you are quite right, she had sixpence! Back went the pennies into the purse.

Then she went to the jeweller's. He lived at the clock-shop, and Gillian loved all the clocks and watches ticking away so busily there. When they chimed and struck all at once she was happier still. First one clock struck the hour, then another and another, until there were twenty at once.

'Is my Mummy's brooch mended?' Gillian asked.

'Yes. I think it is,' said Mr Brown, and he hunted in his big drawer. He took out Mummy's lovely blue brooch. 'Yes, the pin is mended again. I will put the brooch into a little box and you can take it back. Be careful with it, because it is a very nice brooch.'

'Yes, I know,' said Gillian. 'It is Mummy's favourite brooch. Daddy gave it to her one Christmas.'

She watched Mr Brown put the brooch into a tiny box that had white cotton-wool in it. It did look nice there. Mr Brown gave it to Gillian and she put it into her basket.

T—D   97

'How much is that?' she asked.

'Half a crown, please,' said Mr Brown. So once more Gillian opened the purse and took a half-crown out. There was plenty of money left there to take back to Mummy.

Now the basket seemed quite full. There was the butter in it, the parcel of shoes, the box with the brooch in, and the purse. Now just one more thing – she had to ask if Daddy's paper had come.

It had, so that went in at the top of the basket. And now it was time to go home.

'I'll just go past the toyshop on my way home,' said Gillian. 'I haven't got any money of my own to spend, but it would be fun to look in the window, and see if there are any new toys there.'

So she crossed the road very carefully, and went to look in the toyshop. She put the basket down beside her and gazed in at the window. There was a fine new doll there with red hair, dressed in a green frock with green sandals. There was a new ship with a red sail, and a big humming-top sitting by a large box of coloured bricks.

Gillian was so interested in everything that she didn't see a boy coming up quietly behind her. She didn't notice him looking at her basket. She didn't see him picking it up and running off with it!

When at last she turned round to go home, she couldn't see her basket anywhere.

Gillian stared round in dismay. 'Where's my basket?' she cried. 'I put it down here. I know I did! Oh, somebody must have taken it! And it had Mummy's beautiful brooch in it – and her money – and her shoes. Oh dear, whatever shall I do?'

She was so upset. She didn't know whether to go hunting for her basket, or whether to go home and tell Mummy all about it. It was really dreadful.

At last she made up her mind to go home. So with tears in her eyes she set off to tell Mummy how the precious basket had been stolen by somebody.

But I don't know who, thought Gillian. I didn't hear anybody at all. Oh, I do wish Rusty had been with me, then this wouldn't have happened!

Where *was* Rusty? Well, he had wandered up the lane, sniffing at everything. He had gone into the village to see if his friend Rover was anywhere about. Now he was on his way to the butcher's shop to see if any bones had fallen on the floor. He was having a fine time.

Standing looking in at the window of the butcher's was a boy. He was wondering if he should go in and buy some sausages. He was the boy who had stolen Gillian's basket, and he had found the purse inside, and wanted to spend some of the money

The basket was standing beside him. Rusty ran up and sniffed at it. He always sniffed at baskets and boxes.

The more Rusty sniffed the more surprised he was. Woof! he thought to himself. This basket smells just like ours! There's that eggy smell at the bottom where the egg once broke. And there's a smell of the Mistress's shoes. And just here, on the handle is a smell of Gillian's hand. How very strange!

As Rusty stood there sniffing the basket, the boy made up his mind not to buy sausages. So he popped the purse back into the basket, picked the basket up, and went off with it.

Rusty followed him, very puzzled. The boy heard the patter of his feet and shouted at him.

'Go away, dog! Don't follow me like that!'

'Woof!' said Rusty, and went on pattering behind the boy. The boy picked up a stone and threw it. Rusty dodged, and went on scampering behind the boy just the same. He gave a little growl, and this frightened the boy. He didn't throw any more stones.

Woof! thought Rusty. How is it that Gillian has given this bad boy her basket? There is something wrong here.

So he went on following the boy. The boy didn't like Rusty behind him and he began to run. Rusty ran too. The boy ran faster. Rusty galloped along like a small horse. It wasn't a bit of good that boy trying to run faster than Rusty.

At last the boy turned into a yard and ran to a shed, where he meant to hide the stolen basket. He felt in his pocket for the key to open the shed. It had got tangled up in some string and the boy put the basket down to untangle it.

'Woof!' said Rusty, pleased. Quick as light-

ning he took the handle into his mouth and
scampered off with the basket!

'Hi! Hi!' yelled the boy angrily. 'Come back,
you bad dog!'

But you may be sure Rusty didn't come back!

'Stop him! Stop him!' shouted the boy to two
men. 'He's got my basket!'

The two men he was shouting to ran at Rusty.
But he ran through one man's legs and bumped
him over, and he growled so fiercely at the other

that the man was too frightened to touch him.

Down the street ran Rusty, round the corner, and back to the village. Then through the village he went, until he came to the top of the lane. And there he really *had* to put the basket down because it was so heavy! He was only used to carrying it when it was quite empty. Now that it was full it hurt his mouth.

But he wasn't going to give up, you may be sure. So after a bit he picked up the basket again and ran down the lane with it. And who should he meet at the gate of Green Hedges but Gillian! She had just got home and was wondering how to tell Mummy about the lost basket.

'Woof!' said Rusty, making rather a queer sound, because he had the basket in his mouth. 'Woof!'

Gillian turned round. She saw Rusty – and she saw the basket. Her face went red with joy, and she gave a squeal.

'Rusty! You wonderful dog! Where did you get my basket? Oh, how very, very clever of you!'

'Woof, woof!' said Rusty modestly.

Gillian was so pleased with Rusty that she went straight to the butcher's shop and bought him a large juicy bone. He *did* enjoy it!

The white pigeon

'TAKE your baskets and go and find some dandelion leaves for your rabbit,' said Mummy to the twins, Simon and Sally.

'Oh yes, Flop-Ears would like that,' said Sally. 'Come on, Simon, let's go now.'

They took a basket each, and ran out of the garden gate. It was a lovely spring day and the sky was very blue. Big golden dandelions were just coming out everywhere, set in their rosettes of green leaves.

'Flop-Ears will have a good feast today,' said Simon, picking some fresh young leaves. 'He will think it's his birthday.'

They filled their baskets full, and turned to go home again. Then Sally pointed to a bird walking in the road.

'Look! A lovely white pigeon!' she said. 'It's a fantail, isn't it, Simon? See how it spreads its white tail out like a fan!'

The pigeon spread it out beautifully, and then ran to peck at something. It didn't seem to hear a car coming down the lane.

'Mind, pigeon, mind!' cried Simon, but the pigeon didn't get out of the way. The car went right over it.

Sally squealed, but when the car had gone, there was the pigeon, still standing in the road. It looked very frightened.

'The car can't have hurt it!' cried Simon, and ran to the little white bird. It was so frightened that it didn't even run away, or try to fly.

'I think its wing is hurt,' said Sally. 'Look, it's spreading this one, but it can't open the other. Perhaps it *did* get a knock from the car.'

'What shall we do with it?' asked Simon. 'We can't leave it here. If we do, a cat might get it.'

'We'll take it home and ask Mummy what to do,' said Sally. 'How shall we carry it? I don't want to hurt it.'

'I know! I'll put it carefully into my basket, on top of the dandelion leaves,' said Simon. 'It will make a lovely soft bed for it. There, pigeon – are you all right?'

'Coo,' said the pigeon, in a soft little voice. 'Coo-roo-roo.'

'That means it feels comfortable,' said Sally, pleased. 'Oh, doesn't it look sweet in your basket, Simon? I wish I had a pigeon in mine too!'

They went home, carrying the pigeon carefully. It lay very still on the dandelion leaves. The twins went to find their mother, but she was not there.

'Sally, we'd better take it upstairs into the playroom until Mummy comes back,' said Simon. So they took the pigeon upstairs. It tried to get out of the basket.

'Don't struggle, pigeon,' said Sally. 'I'll lift you out gently. Would you like to go into my doll's cot and lie on the soft blue eiderdown?'

The pigeon liked the soft eiderdown and settled down happily in the cot.

'If we shut the door and the window, it will be safe,' said Simon. 'We'd better go and give the dandelion leaves to Flop-Ears before they get dry.'

They shut the window and the door and went downstairs. Flop-Ears was very pleased with the dandelion leaves.

'There's Mummy!' said Sally at last. 'I heard the gate click. Mummy! *Mummy!* We've got something to tell you!'

They took Mummy upstairs to see the little white pigeon. It lay on the eiderdown in the doll's cot, looking at them out of its pink eyes.

'Well!' said Mummy in surprise. 'A pigeon! I met Miss Lacy this afternoon and she told me she had lost her prettiest pigeon. This must be hers!'

'Oh! I was so hoping we might be able to keep it,' said Sally. 'Mummy, I would *so* like a pigeon just like this. Is it hurt, do you think?'

The pigeon suddenly spread both its wings and flew up on Sally's shoulder. 'Coo-roo,' it said. 'Coo-roo!' Sally was so delighted that she couldn't say a word.

But Simon gave a shout and pointed down into the cot. 'Look! Oh do look! It's laid an egg for us on the doll's eiderdown, Sally. Oh Mummy, can we keep the egg? Will it hatch into a baby fantail?'

'Yes. But only if its mother sits on it and keeps it warm,' said Mummy. 'Now, the pigeon seems quite all right. You had better put it into the canary's old cage with its egg, and take it to Miss Lacy. She will be so glad to have it back.'

The twins couldn't help feeling disappointed. They found the old cage, put some straw in it, and then put the pigeon in gently, with its egg. It settled down on it happily.

Simon and Sally carried the cage between them to Miss Lacy. She was pleased to see her pretty white pigeon again!

'How kind of you!' she said. 'And look – it's laid an egg!'

'Yes, it laid it in Sally's doll's cot,' said Simon.

'Did it really? Then it must have wanted to give it to you for being kind,' said Miss Lucy. 'It's *your* egg. So I will let my fantail hatch it, and then when it has grown into a bird, you shall have it for your own, a pretty fantail pigeon just like mine!'

Now every day Simon and Sally go to Miss Lacy's house to see if their egg has hatched yet.

'What shall we call it?' said Simon. 'Snowdrop, I think. Or Snow White? Or perhaps Snowflake?'

Which name would *you* give it if it was your pigeon?

She couldn't go out to play

Susie had been in bed with a bad cold. She was very glad when she was downstairs again, and still more pleased when Mummy said she could go back to school.

'Oh, Mummy, I'm so pleased,' she said. 'If I can go tomorrow I shan't miss the handwork lesson. We always have handwork on Thursdays. I am doing a blue flannel bag for shoes, and on it I am sewing a red railway engine. It looks lovely!'

So the next morning Susie was up at the right time, and ate her breakfast quickly. But what a shock for her when Mummy said, 'Susie, you mustn't go out to play at eleven o'clock this morning, when the others do. You might get another chill. Ask Miss Lesley to let you stay indoors when you've had your milk and biscuits.'

'Oh, Mummy!' cried Susie, with tears in her

eyes. 'I can't stay in at eleven. I *must* go out with the others. It would be dreadful to stay in.'

'Don't be silly, Susie,' said Mummy. 'You don't want to be in bed with another cold, do you?'

'Please, Mummy, say I can go out to play with the others,' begged Susie. But Mummy shook her head.

'It's no use, Susie,' she said. 'You have had a bad cold, and I don't want you to play out of doors today. Either you promise that and go to school, or you don't go to school today at all.'

So Susie promised, but she ran to school crying, for she did so hate to miss her play-time. Miss Lesley saw her red eyes.

'What's the matter, Susie?' she asked.

'Mummy says I mustn't go out to play because I've had a cold,' said Susie.

'Well, never mind,' said Miss Lesley. 'You can tidy the cupboard for me, Susie. That will be a great help. I've wanted to ask someone to do that for me for a long time, but nobody has stayed in.'

So Susie cheered up. But then Alice told

her something that made her feel sad again.

'Do you know, we can't have handwork to-day,' said Alice. 'Isn't it a pity?'

'Why not?' asked Susie.

'Because the key of the handwork cupboard is lost,' said Alice. 'You know, it was always loose in the lock, Susie, and it must have fallen out and got swept up. Anyway, we can't have handwork today because the locksmith can't come till the weekend to open the lock for us.'

Susie was dreadfully disappointed. It would be too bad to have extra arithmetic or dictation instead of lovely handwork.

'Oh dear, I wish I hadn't gone back to school today,' she thought. No play, and no hand-work either. It's too bad!

The morning slipped away. Eleven o'clock came. The children ran out to put on their coats. Soon the playground was full of shout-ing, laughing children. Only Susie was in-doors, looking rather sad. She ate her biscuits and drank her milk. Then she went to the cup-board to start tidying it.

It was really rather fun. There were the piles of exercise books, all new. There was a

box of new pencils, unsharpened, and a box of clean rubbers. There were some new rulers, some notebooks, a box of chalks, and a very untidy corner where all sorts of things had been pushed.

'Oh, here's the little doll that Miss Lesley had to take away from Anne,' said Susie, picking up the little black doll. 'She said she could have it back at half-term, if she was good.

'And here's the penknife we found in the

playground that didn't seem to belong to any-body. And here are three handkerchiefs – what a lot of odd things! I will find a cardboard box and put them all neatly together, then they won't look so untidy.'

Susie got a cardboard box from the cloak-room cupboard and ran back to the classroom with it. She was very happy tidying up the cup-board. It was fun to arrange all the new books and pencils and chalks, and make the shelves look really tidy.

She picked up all the odd things one by one, dusted them, and put them into the box. And, under the pile of oddments, she found a little key. Susie picked it up and looked at it.

'I wonder what that belongs to?' she said. And then a great idea came into her head.

'It might be the lost key of the handwork cup-board! It looks just like it!'

She ran to the handwork cupboard and slipped the key into the lock. She turned it – and the cupboard door opened! It really was the lost key!

What do you think she did next? She knew that in the ordinary way it was handwork after playtime on Thursdays, and that someone usually put out the handwork ready for the children.

I'll give them a surprise, thought Susie excitedly. I'll put out all the handwork; and then when Miss Lesley and the children come back, how surprised and pleased they will be!

So Susie took out the handwork, and, looking at the name on each, she placed each piece of work on the desk it belonged to. She put the box of silks, needles and scissors on Miss Lesley's table. And just as she had finished, the bell rang for the children to come in to work.

Susie slipped into her place. She heard the children in the cloakroom, taking off their coats. And then they came into their classroom.

'I do wish it was handwork now!' said one girl.

'No talking, Anne,' said Miss Lesley. And then all the children saw their handwork on their desks ready for them. How they stared!

'Oh, it *is* handwork!' cried Anne, forgetting she mustn't talk. 'Oh, Miss Lesley, did you find the key of the cupboard?'

'No,' said Miss Lesley, puzzled. 'I can't understand it.' Then she caught sight of Susie's beaming face, and she guessed Susie knew something about it.

'Oh, Miss Lesley, I found the key when I was tidying out the classroom cupboard,' said Susie happily. 'It must have got put in there by mistake. So I unlocked the handwork cupboard, and put out all the handwork for a surprise.'

'Thank you, Susie!' shouted everybody. And Miss Lesley said, 'Well, what a good thing you couldn't go out to play today, Susie, for if you had, we would none of us have been able to do our handwork!'

The flying letter

'DAVID,' said his mother, 'how would you like it if I took you and your cousin Jennie to the circus tonight?'

'Oh, Mummy! Do you really mean it?' asked David. 'Oh, yes, yes – please do! I can tell Jennie at school, can't I?'

'Yes,' said Mummy. 'I'll write a note for her to take home. And as she lives on the other side of the river, and it will be too late for her to go home over the water, she had better stay the night.'

David was very excited. Mr Galliano's circus was a fine one, and he badly wanted to see it. He ran all the way to school that morning, longing to tell Jennie.

But she wasn't at school! David was very disappointed. Miss Brown didn't know why Jennie hadn't come. She had to cross the river to get to school, and her father usually brought her over in a boat and fetched her back, but to-day there was no boat and no Jennie.

David was very upset. However can I let her know about the circus? he thought.

He ran home to tell his mother, when school was over. She was sorry. 'Well, we'll have to go without Jennie,' she said. 'We've no boat to get over the river to her, and it's too wide for you to shout across.'

David ate his dinner gloomily. It was too bad. Jennie didn't have many treats, and now she was going to miss this one.

After dinner he went out into the field that ran down to the wide river. He looked across it to Jennie's house, which stood on the opposite bank. He knew it was no use shouting, for the river was far too wide to carry his voice. If only he had a boat to take him across.

Jennie ran out of her house and waved to David. He waved back. If I put a message into my toy boat the river will carry it away down the middle of the water, and Jennie won't get it, he thought. If only I could think of some way to get a note across!

And then he thought of one. He looked up at

the sky. The wind was very strong and was blowing the clouds from west to east, right across the river.

My kite! thought David. If I get my kite and tie a letter on to the tail and fly it up into the air right across the river, Jennie might get it when it comes down, and read the note. Then perhaps someone will row her across to us and she can go tonight!

He rushed indoors, terribly excited. 'Good gracious!' said Mummy, startled. 'I thought you were an express train, David.'

'Oh, Mummy, I've got such a good idea!' gasped David. 'Where's my kite?'

He pulled it out of the toy cupboard and ran into the garden and out into the field. He shook out the tail and took Mummy's note out of his pocket. Then, very carefully, he made a hole through the letter, ran a piece of string through the hole, and tied the string on to the tail of the kite.

The wind pulled at the kite. David looked to see if Jennie was still there. He saw her, and danced about like a Red Indian, pointing to his kite and then to Jennie. Jennie thought he was

quite mad, but she stood still and watched what he was going to do.

The wind dragged at the kite. The kite wanted to fly on such a breezy day. David threw it up into the air, and paid out the string. The kite tugged and pulled. Its tail hung down and waggled, and the letter swung to and fro.

'Go on, fly high, right over the river!' shouted David. The kite pulled hard and rose above the water. David let out more and more string, hoping that he had enough to get the kite right across the river.

Over it went, flying high. Jennie watched it from the other side. She saw the little square white letter hanging on to the tail, and she wondered what it was.

Now the kite was right across the river, and David had no more string left. He longed for the wind to drop, so that the kite might dive down in circles and drop too. If that happened he didn't mean to tug the kite and get it up high again – he meant to let it fall down, down, down to the grass on the other side of the river, and then maybe Jennie would pick it up and see the letter.

The wind did drop, and the kite dipped down – and down – and down. It made one last wild swoop and struck the grass. David did a dance again, and tried to tell Jennie to pick up his kite. She ran to it, thinking that he wanted her to throw it up into the air again.

She was just going to do so when she saw the letter. On it was written her name – Jennie. She opened the note and read it, and then she understood why David had flown his kite across the river. He had made it carry his message!

How excited she was when she read the note!

She did a dance then, waving her arms about, and then darted home to ask her mother if she could go.

She soon came out with another letter. She tied it on to the kite, and threw it up into the air. The kite rose on the strong wind, waggling its tail and the new note.

And now David began to wind up the string, and bit by bit his kite came across the river, carrying Jennie's note. At last it was right across, and David was able to take the note off the tail and read it.

Dear David,

How lovely! Yes. I can come. Daddy will bring me across at tea-time.

Love from

Jennie

David rushed to show the note to his mother. How she laughed when she heard what he had done that afternoon. 'You deserve to go to the circus,' she said.

These are other Knight Books

J. M. Barrie
PETER PAN AND WENDY

J. M. Barrie's immortal classic has been published in many forms. The text of this edition is one specially retold by May Byron with the author's approval, in order to capture and retain the interest of young children at the time that they are most likely to thrill to the story.

Mabel Lucie Attwell's drawings have become part of the Peter Pan tradition. Never before have all of them appeared in one book. The eight colour plates have been specially selected from the many that she did for *Peter Pan*.

Gwynedd Rae

MOSTLY MARY
ALL MARY

Mary Plain's family are *real* bears, the bears that can be seen in zoos. Mary Plain herself is rather extraordinary and unusual, even for a bear! Her adventures have never before appeared in paperback form, though she has been a top favourite with children and their parents for almost forty years. New illustrations have been specially drawn by Janina Ede.

Ask your local bookseller, or at your public library, for details of other Knight Books, or write to the Editor-in-Chief, Knight Books, Arlen House, Salisbury Road, Leicester, LE1 7QS